Don't Bullshit Me God

Jon Ferguson

Huge Jam

2025

Previously published in this trilogy:

Don't Bullshit Me Daddy 978-1-916604-09-4
Don't Bullshit Me Johnny 978-1-916604-24-7

First published Huge Jam,
Gravenhurst, England 2025

ISBN: 978-1-916604-28-5

FERGUSON'S PREFACE

Once upon a time there was a man… a me… who had lived a long time and had written many books. The "who had lived a long time" is a relative statement of course. Human longevity has changed greatly over the years and will certainly continue to change in the future. But the man was in his seventies in the early twenty-first century, a place he had never imagined being when he was young and when "seventy" seemed very old. But it was here, and he didn't feel very old. The "had written many books" is a less relative statement because he had written some thirty books and as far as he knew that was "many" more than ninety-nine percent of the human population ever writes.

The man decided he had written enough, but, for whatever reason, wanted to write one more and make that last book the most meaningful. Did that mean he didn't think the other books were meaningful? Oh no! Of course not! He thought all his books had worth and value for the world, otherwise he wouldn't have written them. They had not, however, changed the world. And that was what he wanted to do. He wanted the human race to get a different vision of what existence was… is. Whoever invented Christianity had done that. Life under the reign of the Christian religion had millions and millions of people believing that an almighty God had created the world (and the universe for that matter) and if one followed the rules and teachings and had "no other gods before me", etc., one would go to heaven for eternity with God and all the other good people. If not, one would fry in hell or some such thing. Animals and plants were seen to be made for man's consumption, survival, enjoyment, and use. That was what existence was all about. Then came the Age of Enlightenment, Darwin, and democracy. Slowly but surely man began replacing God as having the keys to the bus. Man became "responsible" for the world, not God and the Devil. Man could know the "truth". New bibles were written... not about the Word of God, but the Words of Men. Mankind could bring justice and liberty to the world. Men (and at last women) were said to be created equal and lists of Human Rights began to supersede the divine Ten Commandments. The world was changing for sure, and when the 21st century rolled around, we saw ourselves as being "responsible for the world and even the "climate". Humankind had a new view of itself and the world. God was no longer driving the bus.

The man wanted to bring about another vision of what life was all about... beyond Christianity, beyond humanism and the Enlightenment. He had tried to do this in his other books but, as he was not known outside his region and few readers seemed to understand his message and its importance, he decided to write one more book — his last — called *Don't Bullshit Me God*. It is the final volume of "The Bullshit Trilogy". The first two books – *Don't Bullshit Me Daddy* and *Don't Bullshit Me Johnny* — are written through the eyes of a young girl named Laura Winger. Her beloved mother dies when she is eight, and she and her father are so saddened that they decide to move from California to Switzerland for a new start. Her dear father is dying at the end of *Don't Bullshit Me Daddy*. A year after his death she writes *Don't Bullshit Me Johnny*.

Don't Bullshit Me God is not a novel as such, but a series of glimpses back at the earth through the eyes and perspective of Laura's defunct daddy. Both she and he are somehow closely related to the man… me.

J.F., Morges, 2025

WINGER'S PREFACE

Before getting into the business of this book, I, William Winger, want readers to beware of a headful of wrinkles in my thinking. "Peculiarities" might be a better word than "wrinkles". In any case, I need to make a few things clear about how I see existence.

Firstly, dead after living for nearly seven decades, I have come to the conclusion that it is possible that human beings are not better at knowing what "truth" is — or "reality" — than kangaroos or sparrows are. This might sound like a silly, even absurd, statement. But is it, really? Kangaroos and sparrows have their sense of reality; human beings have theirs. Is either reality "the reality" … real reality? Humans have survived; kangaroos and sparrows have survived. All have dealt with the world with the minds and bodies they were born with. I'm quite sure a kangaroo mind somehow thinks it is "perceiving" reality and truth (of course it probably doesn't use such terms, but I'm sure it is somehow making sense out of the world), just like human minds do. But I believe that neither has a lock on "reality". No one would tell me a kangaroo or a bird could correctly explain the truth of its existence and the reality of the world. I believe that when all is said and done (which, of course, is never), no human being can correctly explain who or what he or she — or anything else — *really* is. Just because we humans have words, doesn't mean we have "truth". Language is no guarantee of truth. In fact, more than anything else, language might hide truth. This is a very difficult idea to grasp because we are all so used to thinking we "know things". *But do we?*

I, the person who has been called "William Winger", believe that reality is far too complex for anyone (except perhaps an all-knowing god, and there very well might not be an omniscient being in the universe) to fully understand, much less describe with words and numbers. For millennia humans all over the world have thought they understood the world. Today it is the same on earth. People think they know what they are talking about. They think "science" today is righting the wrongs of previous generations of "thinkers". And to some extent this might be the case. But I believe that they too are mistaken; however, most humans simply are not lucid, profound, or intelligent enough to understand the limitations of the human mind (through no fault of our own). Humans have great difficulty in realizing that other creatures — like those kangaroos and sparrows — have been able to survive for millions of years without "understanding" existence, without knowing the truth or reality of anything. Might this not be the same for "us" (I include myself, though dead, of course)?

I believe that every moment of life is infinitely complex, and hence unfathomable in any absolute sense. Grasping or chronicling the truth of any single moment is impossible. To accurately describe and understand a single grain of sand, one would have to go back to the beginning of time in order to comprehend how that grain of sand got to be what it is. It goes back millions of years. Maybe billions! Even infinitely! And mightn't things be even more complex for a human being?

(Don't we like to think that we are the most intricate creatures in the cosmos?) In any case, both sand and man go way way back. Maybe forever. Creatures like me believe that there was no beginning of time. We are prone to doubt more or less everything people claim to know, even things as cemented in the human psyche as what a cat is, history, language, the self, Adam and Eve, God, the Big Bang, or who my Aunt Sarah really was...

The second thing I want to warn you about is all the "I"s, "me"s, and "my"s that will inevitably be part of an autobiographical book. In my case, these "I"s, "me"s, and "my"s will be packed with irony and should never be taken too seriously. Why? Because I do not believe there is such a thing as a fixed "I" or a real "me". I am always in flux. At every instant I change. We all do. It is very possible that everything in the universe does. In fact, constant change might be the only certainty in existence. In this text the word "I" will always be used playfully because the author knows that when the chips are down, it — I — refers to nothing real. But he also knows this holds for all words. Language (words) does not "describe" reality; it is part of reality — part of *human* reality. This is crucial to understand if one wants to have a prayer of understanding me. When Descartes declared, "I think, therefore I am," hordes of thinkers all over Western civilization thought he was saying something "true" and "intelligent". I think he was talking nonsense, for precisely the aforementioned reasons, i.e. there is perhaps no fixed "I" that thinks, and it is very possible that it would be far more correct to say, "Thinking exists, therefore it thinks there is an 'I'". No one knows where a thought comes from. No one knows how consciousness functions. No one knows how the "mind" really works. We might "think" we do... But do we really? My "I" doesn't "think" so…

I believe that if everyone were aware of these little details, the world would be a kinder, gentler, more tolerant place. People would be less adamant about their truths and beliefs. Let me just say that it is my prayer… wish… hope… that this book will serve as an example of a kind of thinking that never takes itself too seriously. As I wrote somewhere, "I am just part of a long list of fools who have tried to take the world apart and put it back together again. And we all fail miserably!" Some less miserably than others perhaps, but who really knows?

Here, you might reasonably ask, *Why would someone like me endeavor to write a book… or anything for that matter?* It is a good question and the answer is simple: *Why not?* Just because I don't believe in absolute truth doesn't mean I should shut up. There is no logical connection between not believing in truth and not writing books, not talking to people, and not playing the game of existence. We all — believers, non-believers, truthtellers, doubting Toms — must do something at every instant as long as we exist, even if that something is sitting in a chair or floating on a cloud doing "nothing". It might be argued that creatures like myself would even tend to be more active — e.g. more likely to write books — than "believers" because they have fewer rules and conventions holding them back and keeping them from doing things.

So readers, beware of people like me. But also, beware of yourselves.

To Laura

Don't Bullshit Me God.

by

William Winger

1

Beethoven's 5th Piano Concerto
and the World

So hello… Yes, Winger's the name. William Warren Winger. I was WWW before the internet was invented. (Were my parents visionaries? I don't know, but that world wide web certainly brought some changes to the earth, just like I want to do with this book!). I can't remember anyone ever calling me "Bill". I don't know why, but I was always "William" for them and "William" for my friends at school. Really, my only other appellation was "Daddy". My daughter Laura loved the word so much she put it in the title of her first book, *Don't Bullshit Me Daddy*. Speaking of Laura, I'm proud and happy for her. Proud because somehow, I think she really is one of the few people who are able to get a little perspective on the world. More on that in a minute. And happy for her because I think she has found someone to love. Dead or alive, love has always been one of my favorite themes. I'm so glad my daughter has found a slice of it. As I write, I'm watching her do the dishes with Bernie's kids, Ozzie and Freddie, while he sits in the living room finishing off a bottle of merlot as he listens to Beethoven's 5th Piano Concerto… speaking of which, if you hear Alina Bercu play Beethoven's 5th Piano Concerto accompanied by an orchestra of students from Liszt University, you cannot help but feel that existence is amazing, mysterious, and sometimes incredibly beautiful.

Laura and I used to listen to a lot of wonderful music together. We both realized what good fortune we had to be able to hear whatever music we wanted to, whenever we wanted to, thanks to cassettes, then CDs, then YouTube and Bluetooth, or whatever the hell that technology was called. Up until a century or so ago, the only music human beings could listen to was "live" music.

People are so lucky to be alive today, but most don't seem to agree. They see the world through glasses of pessimism. And why are people pessimistic today? I'd say a big reason is because they have little or no perspective on what the world has been in the past. A perfect example of this is how few people understand that war has always been rampant in this world. The shit in Ukraine and Gaza is nothing new to humanity, and "nothing" compared to the horrors of the past. Yes, the wars in Gaza and Ukraine are horrible, but they are not novel, and they are far from being exceptional. In fact, it seems to be the case that a smaller percentage of people are killed in war on the dear earth today than at any time in known history. People forget what Cortez and Pissarro did to the Aztecs and Incas, i.e. killed about 20,000,000 of them, roughly the same number of human beings killed in World War I. The Napoleonic Wars left 7,000,000 dead. The Manchu Conquest of China (1618-1644) is estimated to have killed 25,000,000. The Punic Wars between the Romans and the Carthaginian Empire two hundred years before Jesus: 1,900,000 dead. The Jewish-Roman Wars around 100 years after Jesus: 1,500,000 dead. There has always been war (and remember, when these wars took place there were far fewer people on earth than there are in the 21st century). And let us not forget the incessant slaughter of animals for human consumption. In your world today some 150,000,000 chickens, pigs, rabbits, and cows meet death *every day* to satisfy your culinary predilections. It's never a nice world, but oh how beautiful it can be… always. Beauty and tragedy are everywhere every second on Earth. When alive, I was neither an optimist nor a pessimist. I simply stood in awe before the mystery of existence. And I also tended to believe that the way a person saw the world was — more than anything — a reflection of his or her self, i.e. happy people see more beauty; unhappy people see more ugliness. I think Laura and Bernie are both happy now. His wife moved in with her lover. Bernie has the kids half the time, and he and Laura pretty much have each other all the time.

I have often wondered how Beethoven stood with regard to Napoleon. Did he see the French general as part of the beauty or the horror? Was the Fifth Concerto a homage? If I ever bump into Ludwig Van, I'll ask him what he thought. If I ever bump into Napoleon, I'll ask him how he felt about the music and, in retrospect, if he sees himself as a hero or villain. Who knows, maybe he has a different perspective now... here... where he and I and Ludwig are, all ethereal and naked with no flesh to clothe, in some godforsaken corner of the cosmos, where, by the way, the absence of music is a killer! Wasn't it Nietzsche (remember, I had degrees in both philosophy and business, which in itself made me a rather curious human being) who said, "Life without music would be a mistake." Well, there is none here. At least I haven't encountered any yet. All we do really is ruminate.

Once, I was floating on a cloud and thinking about the origin of my love for Laura's mother, my beloved wife. A week passed and I was still thinking about why I loved her teeth. A month passed and I hadn't yet understood why I loved her eyes. Then the year elapsed and I was still putting the lines and dots together to explain why I loved the shape of her face. A slice of infinity passed, and I finally had a hint as to why I loved the way she touched me. A slice later, I sensed I was beginning to understand why I loved her mind. I've been in heaven now for who knows how long, and honestly, I still don't know why I loved all of her. The other day I was explaining all this to Isaac Newton and he said it was really just a question of gravity. It made sense to me.

It is strange that I still haven't bumped into her here. Newton yes; my beloved wife no. I am still hoping.

When I think about my daughter Laura, everything I shared with her had been intended to do more than just amuse her. I had wanted to get her to see "life" in a different way, and, in so doing, make the world a better place, at least her world that is. Part of the "see 'life' in a different way" was to get her to realize that we are all essentially prisoners of our moment in history and the culture and weltanschauung into which we are hatched. At the same time, I tended to doubt all people who thought there was a logic or intrinsic meaning behind existence. I believed everything was what it was and couldn't be anything other than what it was at any moment in time, a belief I still maintain and think its promulgation to be the key to a better world.

I realized that people really never change much and their minds are, more often than not, stuck in ruts with blinders that make it very difficult to see new ways of viewing the world inside and outside. "Inside and outside" of what? The human head of course. Or perhaps we should call it "the mind". Ostensibly, there is what is inside the mind and what is outside the mind. But is this true? Is the mind a "thing" that is separate from the rest of the world? Is it an identifiable thing? Perhaps the mind is constantly changing as it relates to and deals with the world "outside". Perhaps it cannot be separated from the world outside. And a greater question might be, "Has anyone in history ever fully grasped or understood what a mind is and how it works?" One thing is certain: different minds have different views of reality and the world. Different cultures create different explanations for what "life" is and what existence is all about. Seemingly, all people and all cultures think their vision of the world is correct. I observed this all my life and I tried to get Laura to see it too. We watched people and civilizations create values and judge each other as being good and evil, guilty and not guilty, in possession of truth or untruth — all thinking their judgements about the world were correct. Throughout my whole terrestrial existence I observed categorical people who claimed to know what life was about, what reality was, who was guilty and who was innocent, and how things "should" be. And the result was the world as it was and still apparently is…

I tried to get Laura to imagine a world wherein no one claimed to know the truth about what life was all about, no one claimed to know what reality was, no one saw himself or herself to be in a position to judge guilt and innocence or the why or wherefore of what went on in the world, and people were finally beginning to realize that is was very possible that absolutely nothing in existence could be other than what it was at every moment in time. I wanted her to realize that if people really understood this, the world would be a very different place, one of mystery, awe, wonder, openness, and compassion. I think Laura at least got my message.

O Earth, how I miss you sometimes…

2

What Is a Human Being?

I used to often feel that I was not part of the world. It was sometimes a depressive feeling, other times a lonely feeling, but not infrequently an ecstatic feeling. In any case, it led my mind (or was it the mind that had led the feeling?) in many different directions.

One direction was wondering what human beings really were… are. I would often walk down the street and suddenly sense that I had no idea what the creatures around me were. I think most people tend to spend their lives thinking they know what a human being is. Is this an error? Might they be deeply mistaken as to what people are?

Way back when, I was raised thinking that human beings were children of God and somehow created in His image. This made them creatures of the highest order. They all had my utmost respect. When I stopped believing in the God (and gods), my teachers and peers insisted that human beings were at the top of an evolutionary process. This kept human beings in a rather positive light, higher than apes and rodents. Eventually, I doubted both the children of God idea and the evolutionary hierarchy. So, what were human beings?

As far as I knew, no one in Western civilization had come up with a good third or fourth or fifth possible explanation. Perhaps in the Orient there reigned a cloudy mysterious answer that might have attracted me. But there I was, in the West, hearing what went on around me. Who talked about another possibility other than divinity's children or the monkey business?

I remember sometimes walking down the street and laughing out loud. What are all these two-legged creatures around me? What am I? What do we have in common? What don't we share? Should we be considered part of one great big family? Or are some of us very different? Are we all different? Should I give more credence and respect to these two-legged creatures than I do to other four-legged, six-legged, eight-legged, hundred-legged, legless, slithering or flying creatures? If so, on what grounds?

Great was my sense of wonder and ecstasy. Even back then I had a feeling of floating — inside, outside, above, below — like I myself was an ethereal "human" cloud.

I could be walking to the post office. If passersby could have read my mind, surely some of them would have thought I had to go to the nearest psychiatric clinic. But no! No! I had to pay my bills. I always paid them early to avoid waiting in line with hordes of other two-legged creatures. Only we humans paid bills! Only we were so blessed and honored! Only we had nut houses for the mentally deranged!

As I float here now and think about the creatures I knew and observed on the earth, I wonder how we should have viewed each other... As equals? Unequals? Fraternally? Lovingly? Cunningly? Cunnulinically (new word)? Savagely... socially, tenderly, warmly, coldly, intellectually, instinctively, emotionally, rationally, irrationally, scientifically, religiously, sentimentally, brutally, materialistically, spiritually, superficially, profoundly, fatally, innocently, philosophically, spatially, temporally, eternally, finitely, infinitely...?

I wondered much about the human race and in many ways. I had thoughts oozing with compassion, forgiveness, and understanding. Other times, humankind — including myself of course — seemed so petty, hopeless, boring, ugly, and insignificant. Then suddenly people would appear to be so ingenious, creative, brilliant, and beautiful!

But I must be honest: I had the same kind of thoughts about animals, insects, plants, flowers, trees, rocks, landscapes, clouds, rainbows, moons, planets, stars, galaxies, and so-called black holes. What were they? How should they be perceived and judged? Eyes, ears, hands, fingers, consciousnesses, and "brains"... that was what we had to perceive and judge with. Was it enough? Had we reason to trust it all? Had we any choice?

So, I still ask, what is a human being? Is it possible for one to perceive and judge itself? Aren't their biases *a priori* and extreme? Don't they forget that when they judge themselves, they are the ones making up the rules? Could an eagle know what an eagle is? Could it accurately judge itself? Could an ape, an ant, or a fish?

I suggest that honesty will force reflective people to admit that they have no idea what they are. Human beings will never be able to look at themselves in the mirror and know what they're seeing. But they will continue to pretend they do. They will continue to be satisfied with answers like "children of God" or part of an "evolutionary chain".

But they are mysteries, like everything else. And the sooner they admit it the better. Admitting it will be like bringing champagne to the party. Good champagne. The top of the line…

3

To the Moon and Back

Obviously, I've never been able to turn off the machine. I couldn't even walk upstairs without my mind going to the moon and back. But what the hell was I supposed to do? That was the way I was. I still am for that matter, still part of the nothing-can-be-other-than-what-it-is and still thinking about the nature of reality and how humans perceive it. Newton and I spoke about that little gem-of-a-subject not long ago, and it turns out we were of the exact same opinion. With a grin he said, "All being is what it is and can be nothing other... It's as obvious as the sun." And then we started conversing about the way earthlings see life and death as opposites, and we agreed that it was a perfect example of how the human head bumbles as it goes about things. In this case, thinking that there are opposites in the universe — "long and short", "big and small", "intelligent and stupid", "high and low" ... and "life and death". These aren't opposites. They are just part of continuums in an infinite cosmos. Thinking they define reality is about as absurd as a world without music...

...Speaking of which, I ran into my friend Mr. Nietzsche the other day. Not only did we talk about life without music being an error (Heaven's error?), but also about how essentially all human thinking is an "error".

Since blowing my brains out, I've been haunted by the idea that words and thoughts simply do not... cannot... describe "reality". All they ever do is describe a jumbled human perception of reality. Perhaps the most ridiculous dichotomies in human discourse are correct-erroneous, right-wrong, and true-false! It is easy to see that there is no absolute big-small, high-low, up-down, inside-outside, or even beautiful-ugly in the reality of a potentially infinite universe, but it is much more difficult to understand the possibility that the "correct-erroneous" dichotomy exists only in the human head and has no real meaning outside of it. Why? Because the correctness (truth, rightness) of something is always a "human" judgement that is based on a human perspective and perception of the world. To say that "Paris is a beautiful city" or "Paris is the capital of France" are statements that make sense... are "correct"... for human beings. For an eagle or a cow or a dolphin (or a "god"?) these statements mean absolutely nothing. There is no such thing as "Paris" or a "capital city" or even "beauty" for that matter. These are all human constructs. Even the truth of the statement "1 + 1 = 2" only makes sense in a "human" vision of reality, where is it presumed that the universe can be divided into distinct "fixed" parts? It makes perfect sense for humans, but probably means nothing to any other creature in the universe. Mathematics is part of our vision of reality. But is our vision correct? And is there a "correct" way to see existence? We humans would never say an eagle's perception of the world is "correct"; we would simply say it is the eagle's way of seeing reality. Ditto for dolphins, cows, dogs. But not for humans! We believe our way of seeing the world is accurate... correct... valid... true. But at the same time, we forget that we are the ones who have created the possibility that truth, accuracy, validity, wrongness, falsity, and untruth exist in the universe. We are the ones who have invented the dichotomy "correct-erroneous". We are the ones who have created the possibility that something... anything... in the universe is "right" or "wrong". We constantly make judgements about the so-called truth of essentially everything. (In all likelihood, eagles, dolphins, cows, and dogs don't do any such thing.) And why do we do this? Because that is the way we are... what we are, i.e. we are the creatures that crown ourselves kings and queens of the jungle. We think we are the only creatures (other than the "gods" we invent... usually in our own image, of course!) that are capable of seeing existence... any part of existence... correctly! We would never say a dolphin sees the world correctly. If anything, we would say it sees it instinctively based on the brain and eyes that it has. But why don't we say that about ourselves? Why don't we admit that we too are stuck with minds, brains, eyes, and noses that have evolved to where they are today, which is certainly not to the "truth"! Why? Because we, too, are limited and are blind to the unfathomable mystery and complexity of Being. Put another way, if nothing in the universe is fixed… if everything is always changing (as modern physics seems to be telling us)… then are not all our judgements about reality skewed?

Yes, human beings spend their whole lives actually believing they can be — and are — "right" about things and that they can see the world "correctly". Does one need to be "dead" to see what a preposterous supposition this is? Who on earth can step back, look at the universe, and see the absurdity of the human mind thinking it sees the world "correctly"? Who can imagine that the human vision of reality is limited just like that of the eagle and the dolphin? Who can imagine that human brains and eyes also act instinctively based on all the experiences their ancestors have had? Who can imagine that it is nowhere written in gold that the human mind can see things correctly and that the dichotomy "correct-erroneous" has no more "truth" to it than the up-down dichotomy does? … Ah! The dead man, that's who!

Everywhere human beings turn, other human

beings are telling them how things are, what is true and what isn't, what is correct and what is erroneous. This is the human way. To do otherwise is to be an animal. Or perhaps, who knows, a god?

4

Nowhere To Go

Which statement is closer to the truth... People are free to go wherever they want... or... They have nowhere to go...?

Let us look at the first idea: People are free to go wherever they want. Obviously, this is patently false because none of them can go to Mars and most of them can't go to the moon or even Honolulu or Venice (because of time and/or financial restrictions, etc.). So, if we look out at the universe, people certainly can't go to 99.99999% of it. If we look at the earth, most people have a good number of choices, but few, if any, can go wherever they want.

But the original statement talked about going wherever "they want" to go. Where do most people want to go? Certainly not to Mars, but rather to the grocery store, to sit in front of a TV, to the toilet, to Paris or Disneyland, to McDonald's, to a friend's house or a whorehouse, or to the opera or a football game. In these cases, where they want to go will be determined by their life situations, their predilections, and their desires. So, what determines those things? How much say do "they" have in who they are and their situation in this world. Of course, most of them would immediately respond by saying they are highly responsible for their lives, their situations, their preferences, and their desires, in spite of the obvious fact that none of them asked to be born where they were born with the body and mind that they have. Of course, once they are born, little by little they may have a say in who they turn out to be, but when this might actually begin is certainly rather foggy.

The more I thought about my initial question, the more I began to feel that people all go where life takes them, but this will not necessarily be where they want to go and if it is where they want to go, there is no certainty that their "wants" were freely formed, but rather came from a mind and body that they themselves had little or no control over.

When you look at a hill of ants, with all the creatures doing what they do, do you ever think they are doing what "they want" to do? I didn't. I think they are doing what they are "programmed to do" (not by any other higher being, but simply by what they happen to be!) and that they have probably no "choice" whatsoever about their movements and destinations. Now, when you are in a helicopter or at the top of a tall building and you look down at the herds of people scurrying around in the city below, do you not also wonder if they too might be doing what they "are programmed to do" (not by any other higher being, but simply by what they happen to be!)? I didn't.

To make a long story short, I began to wonder if most creatures on earth, including humans, really have nowhere to go except where they happen to be going — for an infinity of reasons that no one will ever understand — at every single solitary unique moment of their lives. It's an interesting thought: the idea that, in spite of the appearance of things, we are all prisoners of "who we are" and the anthill on which we find ourselves and, hence, are all trapped in cages with… nowhere to go. Even me and Sir Isaac…

5

Levity

I'm sure Laura would agree that I tried to keep even the weightiest subjects light. I always tried to toss in a little humor. Like the anthill. But the longer I'm here, the more I think that it is just that... *an anthill*. The difference being that the ants are probably less cruel to each other than the humans, although as I recall, ants do sometimes fight, protect their territory against other ant groups, etc. Evidently, they even get into fights when it comes to mating games. All this sounds strangely familiar, and more proof of my thesis that nothing can be other than what it is.

O this godforsaken universe! *But was God ever here to forsake anything?*

6

History

Much is said about human intelligence. Examples abound that most people accept as proof of human brain power: inventions like the wheel and electricity, Plato, alphabets, trips to the moon, Aristotle, Jesus, architectural techniques, Augustine, washing machines, pyramids, skyscrapers, Leonardo DaVinci, atomic bombs, Michelangelo, certain vaccines, heart transplants, cars, toilets, Galileo, Newton, airplanes, Einstein, computers, iPhones… As a race, humans are convinced that we are the most intelligent creatures in the known cosmos. And if not there, at least the smartest beasts on earth.

But what about our stupidity? Is enough said about that? Are we honest with ourselves? Are we able to see both sides of the coin? Are we able to judge our ignorance with equal force and energy as we do our intelligence? Let us take a moment and look at human stupidity and some of its greatest examples. When we finish, perhaps we can ask the question, *When all is laid out on the table, do the scales tip more to the side of lucidity or obscurity, intelligence or stupidity?*

But won't we always be prejudiced in our judgements? Won't we always see ourselves through tinted or tainted glasses? Aren't we always the ones making the rules about what constitutes intelligence or ignorance? Don't we always rely on our own value systems to make our judgements? And here, haven't we already hit on one of the greatest proofs of human stupidity — the fact that one is rarely, if ever, able to see, admit, and understand that one's judgements are always at the mercy of one's mind and world view?

I am no longer part of the earth. I might have a more objective view. Haha! In any case, here are a few propensities that might best reveal the human lack of intelligence...

As a species, you tend to kill your own kind more than most other creatures do. And you kill each other for a rainbow of reasons. Yes, perhaps certain animals kill each other at a higher rate than humans do, but no creatures kill each other with your vigor and tenacity. You have cannons, blades, rockets, missiles, atomic bombs, Kafelnikovs, poison gases, machine guns, Colt 45s (just this weekend I saw that 63 people were shot in the city of Chicago alone). You murder, you pillage, you assassinate, you have wars, you drop bombs, you spray napalm, you plough cars and trucks into crowded markets, you fly airplanes into mountainsides, you even kill each other for sport (O

how some of you must miss those Roman gladiators —
certainly far more entertaining than American football
or boxing!). You kill in the name of God, truth, and
freedom (are the dead ever free?). So, I ask: Are there
many things on earth that are dumber than this?

A second example of gross human stupidity is that
in spite of all the information you now have about
myriad religious beliefs all over the world — all
claiming to be "true" — people still have an
overwhelming tendency to believe that "theirs"
(usually the one they were raised in) is the only one
that is really, really the truth! More than half of the
world's population believes in either the Christian
religion or the Moslem religion. Another billion or so
believe in other gods. All tend to believe they are right
and the others are wrong, though the odds are that all
are wrong. Is this not a sign of trans-stupidity? Or at
least a manifestation of massive weakness of some
kind?

And now to the title of this chapter — "History"!
Mightn't the global belief in the possibility of
comprehending — and writing — history not be the
greatest proof of all of our bluntness and overall dull-
headedness as a species? We are most certainly the
only species that pretends to record history, to know
history, and to understand history. Isn't this a huge
fantasy? Many animals "learn" from events that occur
in the past (if I pee again on the kitchen floor I'll get
smashed in the nose with a newspaper!) and certainly

all creatures (including, and perhaps especially, humans) have a set of instincts that have been formed over millions and millions — even billions (infinity anybody?) — of years on the earth, but humans are the only creatures who purport to have "knowledge" of history and who write thousands of books about "what happened" in the past... "The History of Mankind", "The History of France", "The History of Chinese Pottery", "The History of Art", "The History of the American Indian", "The History of Rome", "A History of Fishing", "The History of Boxing", "The History of Ancient Greece", "The History of Sex", "The History of the Automobile", and on and on. In every case, someone is making a noble effort to "explain" part of what has gone on in the world in the gigantic "past". Of course there is nothing intrinsically bad about making such efforts, but how naïve it is to think that you can capture even 0.00001 % of what actually "happened" at any moment in life.

What do I mean? This: Every moment on Earth (every moment of existence) is infinitely complex... mind-bogglingly complex! Stop and think. Right now. This moment. Think of the infinite complexity of your body. Billions of cells... moving, changing, developing. Even the greatest physician (medical doctor or physicist) in the world could never explain "you" at any given moment. "You" are a mystery beyond comprehension. And yet... and yet you will use one little word — "you" — and you will use one littler word — "I" — and we will all be satisfied thinking you know what you are talking about. But the truth is, when any of us say "you" or "I", we have absolutely no idea what we are talking about! And yet we think we do! The same is true with the cat at your feet, with the tree outside your window, with Donald Trump, George Washington, Genghis Khan, Jesus, Mary Poppins, a fly, a mouse, God, the sun, and your old Aunt Milly... essentially every thing in the universe. We think we know what things are! But every instant is infinite... infinitely complex... "beyond infinity". Our stupidity comes from the fact that we do not recognize this. 99.99 % of us think we know what we're talking about. For millennia now we have been breaking up the world with language and concepts and putting it back together again such that it makes perfect (or almost perfect) sense to us all. Not only do we think we know what's going on in the present (Oh look, Peter is unhappy. It must be because his girlfriend left him...), but we even try to explain the past... history... the infinity of infinitely complex moments before the present! Imagine the task of explaining a world war when one can't even understand oneself! But we do it constantly. All the time. Everywhere. All over the world. We explain the present, the past, and even talk about what will happen in the future and why. And of course, we think we're making sense. We have cut the world up a certain way (knowing nothing definitive about anything) and we put it back together with concepts and language and everybody is satisfied and thinks that they are talking about "reality".

You humans all have "your world". You believe it is real and that you more or less know how it functions, what is going on now in the present, and what went on in the deep dark depths of "history". You are believing creatures. You organize your beliefs in a myriad of ways. Your beliefs are surely as necessary as blood and rain for your survival. But believing something does not make it true.

The French have one word for two different things: "histoire". It can mean "history" or "story". A "story about history" would be "une histoire sur l'histoire". Maybe they are on to something, i.e. that history is simply a wonderful story... the greatest story of all... but a consummate fairy tale just the same.

7

Love, Freedom, and the Keys to the Bus

I love all this… and my freedom to talk about it. Did I sense it while I was on Earth? To an extent, for sure. But not like I do now. It took death for me to realize the full impact. I used to know brilliant mathematicians who believed in malarkey like miracles, visits from outer space, gods and prophets, and who were religious fanatics. The same mind can be highly rational and highly irrational. But in the end, what is reason? What is logic and rationality? Who really does have the keys to the bus? I've been looking for such a being ever since I got here, just like I did while on the twirling earth. Niente. Nada. Haven't found anything. And it's not because I haven't been looking.

8

Getting Along in the World

*To accuse others for one's own misfortunes is a sign of
lack of education. To accuse oneself shows that one's
education has begun. To accuse neither oneself nor
others shows that one's education is complete.*

—Epictetus

As I used to tell my daughter Laura (I remember talking about it during our trip through the Black Forest), in a civilized society people are good at finding ways of getting along with each other. And that means trying to understand each other, forgiving each other, and being open to new ways of seeing and understanding situations. Most wars are the opposite of all this. Both sides blame the other and want to "punish" the other and seek "revenge". Both sides see themselves as "victims".

I always believed that a good way to judge a society was to look at how many people felt that they were victims. The fewer the "victims", the better the society. A civilized world would try to get as many people as possible to feel good about themselves. Being pitied and feeling victimized is never a "good" way to feel. Victims rarely, if ever, feel strength. And isn't feeling strong always better than feeling weak?

Sadly, before I left the world, much of Western civilization seemed to be trying to create as many victims as possible. Victims tend to see the world in a negative way, as a nasty place. People who feel good about themselves are more prone to see the world as a nice place. When on Earth I never tried to make someone feel like a victim; I tried to make people understand the complexity of the world and figure out ways to make the best of what remained of one's life. I think Laura and Bernie are the same way. I remember watching how they helped Laura's pregnant friend, Natasha. They didn't pity her; they helped her find a way to solve her problem of an unwanted pregnancy.

More than two millennia ago Epictetus gave people some good advice about how to see the world by telling them to stop blaming each other and start understanding each other in order to get along and bring as much joy to life as possible. I think he and I both sensed that neither ants nor people could be other than what they were. This little thought opened some big windows on the world.

9

The Most Preposterous Idea

Yes, it finally dawned on me, not long before I blew my brains out. I called it "The Most Preposterous Idea". It took a long time for it to appear clearly in my mind. But when it did, it rang loudly and clearly, kind of like a song that one can't get out of one's head. It went something like this…

"Ladies and gentlemen of the world, there are twice two possibilities:

Either existence was created or it wasn't.

Either there are supreme forces and intelligences behind existence or there are not.

To both of these queries our civilization — our great Western civilization — has been very clear, and our tender human brains have been bombarded with these answers:

Yes, existence was 'created', and yes, there are supreme 'forces' and 'intelligences' behind existence.

Not only that, but implicit in both of these answers is

the idea that existence exists 'for a reason', and hence, there are always answers to questions as to 'why' this or that exists and 'why' this or that happens…

Our civilization is completely based on two groups of people: the 'Greek thinkers' before Christ and the 'Christian thinkers' after Christ. These two groups left us with the foundations of our view of ourselves, the world, and the cosmos. Essentially everything we 'think' comes from them, even what 'thinking' itself is, e.g. we humans think 'freely', but animal thinking is 'instinctive'.

Plato and his friends believed in gods that created and controlled the world. In fact, these gods were much like us humans, only more powerful and more intelligent.

Then the Christians and Muslims came along and told us that there was only one God, but that He was all-knowing and all-powerful.

In any case, existence had a 'reason', a 'purpose', and a 'logic'. It came from somewhere, from 'God' or gods (today, of course, we also have the Big Beautiful Bang as an explanation), and, perhaps more importantly, 'man' was special, i.e. just below God, and all the rest of existence was called 'nature' (animals, plants, etc.).

This separation of Man from Nature led to a whole slew of other wild ideas, for example, a) that the human brain (because we are just below God in intelligence) can know the 'truth' about the world, and b) that so-called 'nature' has some kind of harmonious balance to it because it was created by a perfect Being… a "God".

Look around you today. Listen to people talk. This

vision of existence dominates the way we see more or less everything.

Who do you know who says that existence was not created?

Who says existence has no intrinsic meaning, purpose or goal, nor a higher power behind it with a 'plan' or a 'design'?

Who says that human beings — and everything we do — is absolutely part of nature and that the human mind is NOT equipped to 'understand' existence?

Who declares that everything on earth is absolutely 'natural' and part of NATURE?

And finally, who do you know who feels the absolute mystery of all existence at every moment?"

That was my song, and the more I thought about it, the more I believed that separating man from nature was far and away the most preposterous idea in the history of Western civilization. It opened the gates for an enormous flood of illusions about our way of seeing and feeling existence... ideas like: Nature cannot be "evil"; only humans can be evil. Nature is not free and can never be other than what it is. Only humans are free and when they do something bad ("evil"), they "deserve" to be punished! Justice must be served! There is no justice in nature, but only in the human arena. By punishing or imprisoning the "bad" parts of humanity, we in the Western world think we create a "just" world. Take revenge on this person or those people and the scales have been balanced…

But now I see it from afar. There are no scales to be balanced. All existence is what it is. When all existence is seen to be "natural" and one understands that nothing can be other that what it is (including oneself), the world becomes a different kind of Eden. Not an eternal perfect Garden of Eden created by some kind of perfect mind, but rather everything that we see, i.e. a great stage… a kind of playground or park or zoo full of a vast variety of amazing creatures… a theatre of power where parts of nature dominate other parts, where parts destroy other parts, where parts bring joy and happiness, where parts are bigger, stronger, and more creative than others, where parts are kinder and gentler than others, where parts believe in this and that and other parts in that and this and sometimes they get along and sometimes they don't.

Now, from afar, I see the world very differently. I had glimpses when I was alive. But now that I am dead, I realize that all parts of existence are as natural as all other parts.

10

*A Question
No One Seems to Ask*

I've been thinking about a question, and the more I think about it, the more I believe it might be one of the most interesting philosophical questions in the cosmos. It is this: If we can ever find a Supreme Being, if God exists, COULD HE (SHE or IT) BE OTHER THAN WHAT HE (SHE or IT) IS? If not, then wouldn't God also be part of nature and just like every other part of the whole shebang, i.e. condemned to be what it is?... (Don't you love that word, "shebang"? So much nicer the "hebang" or "itbang"!) — Imagine if all beings, including Supreme Beings, had no choice in being what they were and all were as much a part of nature as pinecones, blueberries, English muffins, frogs, and the Super Bowl! Imagine if even the most powerful being in the universe had no choice in being what it was? Wouldn't this change everything about how power was perceived, be it a god, a sun, a Roosevelt, a Churchill, a Napoleon, a Trump, a Putin, a Macron, an earthquake or a typhoon? If power can be nothing other than what it is, all of what we have on Earth and in the cosmos, is absolutely normal and natural. Is this a frightening thought? A saddening one? A tragic one? Or might it even be a thought that could bring joy to the whole shebang… even a kind of ecstasy? Ah! Cosmos, dear cosmos, perhaps you have tricked us up until now, but finally we are beginning to see through you!

Ah! All good thoughts and questions for a rainy day… except it doesn't rain here. Speaking of which, when I think about all the ungrateful bastards back on Earth who used to bitch and complain about rain! Such silly unthinking fools… No rain, no life!

In any case, here in my current cubbyhole, I've got plenty of time to think. It's interesting that I put to use my philosophy studies far more than all the business courses I took. But I'll admit, when I was on Earth, I was amazed at what businesses were able to create and overall, how well the world functioned. So many people used to see the glass half empty, but I always tended to see it half full, appreciating all the progress in so many domains.

11

Seeing the World in a New Way

I'm not ashamed to admit it — my goal is to get people — all people everywhere — to see the world in a different way. This way: We never blame nature; we accept it and do the best we can to deal with it. We don't hate nature; we accept it, deal with it as well as we can, and move on. We accept it because we know it can be nothing other than what it is. We never want revenge on nature because we know nature is innocent. It cannot be blamed for being what it is. So, if we put mankind back into nature, it will radically change the way we see each other and our lives on this earth.

I, William Winger — long dead, but somehow still part of Being — saw, and continue to see, human beings and all human activity exactly the way I see the rest of the world, i.e. as part of "nature". Everything, absolutely everything, is part of the natural universe. Humans are a different part, an interesting part, but not "outside" of nature. As I have said, I believe separating us from nature was the greatest intellectual error in the history of Western civilization. Saying that we were "free" (and the rest of existence was not) created a totally false idea of what men and women were and are. Saying people are "responsible" — and trying to get them to feel responsible — is a wholly different issue. Of course, we must be made to feel "responsible", just like a dog needs to feel responsible not to pee on the living room carpet. But the reality is that a human being is no more "responsible" for being what he or she is than a dog or any other part of existence. I repeat: no one asked to be born; no one asked to have the mind and body she or he has; no one selected the society and circumstances into which they were born. Nothing in existence asked to exist. It all just is, including humanity and everything humanity does. The myth of "free will" is a blight on the earth. It gives us a distorted idea of existence. It creates hate and vengeance and wars. Yes, it must be overcome — surpassed — in order for the world to truly become a better place. My mission is to get people to understand this. I am not free. I am simply one of those creatures that wants to see as much joy and love as possible, and as little war and hate as possible.

Yes, I want to change the world; I want to bring more peace, innocence, and understanding to the world. Yes, I tried in my own way when I was on Earth. And yes, I ended up blowing my brains out. But that wasn't because I thought I had failed. No, it was because of the pain I had. That damn pancreatic cancer got the best of me. And no, I did not want to be a burden to my dear daughter Laura. And yes, I think she understood, and as I write, I sense that she is loving life.

12

What Is Life?

It is time to make as clear as possible how I, William Warren Winger, see "life". But first, what is it?

I believe that no one knows what "life" is, and yet almost every human being I have ever known seems to think he or she knows what life is. I don't. Every second on Earth was a mystery to me. Every bit of existence, from the smallest quark or electron to the biggest creature or mass, is part of that mystery.

Somewhere I read a sentence I've never forgotten: "Where did the mystery go? To sleep in the bed of knowledge."

Yes, humans think they "know" things. Like all conscious creatures, humans have a "world" and they navigate in that world. It is only natural that all creatures make sense of their world. Humans are no different. The history of humanity is the history of different ways of seeing the world (and universe). There have been different "realities" all over the planet. And of course, every society thinks "its" reality is the real reality! It is perfectly normal for people to "think" they know what reality is and how the world works. That is the human way. But that does not mean any group or person actually "has" the truth. We all have a sense of reality; but actual truth is something I believe no one has.

Few people share this vision with me. I have no idea as to how I came to see the world this way. But I did. I believe no human being understands how his or her own mind works, much less the mind of another human being or creature. Of course, people think they do, but I believe no human mind understands where its "thoughts" come from and how its consciousness works. Where is it written in the universe that the human being — with a human mind — has the innate capacity to understand the cosmos? We don't think other creatures on Earth are able to do so, so why do we think we can? Can't we accept the fact that our minds and brains are not equipped to get to the bottom of Being? Can't we realize that all-knowing divinities are an invention of the human mind and that we, in all likelihood, will never be such beings and will never understand existence? And can't we realize that the world was not "made for us" and has never been some kind of "Garden of Eden"? Can't we understand that the human head constantly simplifies "reality" — all reality all the time? There is nothing wrong with this. Seemingly, we cannot do otherwise. We are condemned to make sense of the world if we want to live in the world. And from Neanderthal "people" to Wall Street "people", to Buddhists, popes, priests, and rocket scientists, we all construct a vision of reality that makes perfect sense to each of us. Putin's reality makes perfect sense to him. Biden's reality makes perfect sense to him. So do Trump's and Hillary Clinton's. So did Hitler's, Heidegger's, Florence Nightingale's, Stalin's, Churchill's, Einstein's, Gandhi's, Truman's, Kennedy's, and the Dalai Lama's. Can't we understand that every human makes sense of the world in his or her own way? But who has the "correct" way? Who knows what "life" is and how it functions? Who has the truth? No one that I know of...

...But we can all guess. And I, William Winger, have a best guess that says that nothing — including mankind — was created by a "God" or gods. Accordingly, I believe nothing was created "for a reason". Not man, not earths and galaxies. Not ants and snakes and trees and plants. All existence simply is. And it is always in flux. And it has no rhyme or reason because there is nothing behind life, behind existence. And I also intuit that all existence is "life". For me, Being and life are eventually — finally — synonymous. There would be no "life" on earth without Being, without existence. To think man and plants and animals are the only things that are alive makes no sense. How can humans — who live a piddling eighty or a hundred years at best — think they are "life", and that the sun — which has existed for billions of years and without which no creature on earth would exist — is NOT "life"? How can we be so petty and blockheaded? So anthropomorphic?

I'll tell you why. Because we think we are special. First, we thought we were God's children! Then — today — many of us think we are at the top of some evolutionary totem pole. Neither is true. But in both cases, we have always thought we were special. And yes, we are special. But so is every other creature on earth, and every sun and star and planet! All Being is special! All beings are special! All is miraculous! And all is "nature"!

And my best guess is that the idea of a "creation" or a "beginning" makes no sense at all. I believe existence has always existed…all of it. It simply (or infinitely complexly) changes constantly. But I believe Being itself has always been. And that leads me to my most radical thought, the most difficult thought of all: Nothing at any given moment can be other than what it is. Nothing in the universe is "free". But beware! This does not mean that things are "predestined" to be what they are. This does not mean things are "determined". No, I don't believe there is some Jolly Green Giant behind existence that has decided how things will be. Existence simply is what it is… All of it — absolutely all of it! Nothing was predestined. Everything simply is. And none of it can ever be other than what it is at any given moment. Of course, things change, including people and their minds, bodies, and consciousnesses. Existence is a flow. But not a free flow, because "free" implies that there is a "free will" behind it… A "will", yes. But not a will that can be other than what it is. Here is the catch! And it is all a mysterious flow that no human mind or dinosaur mind or eagle or ant mind will ever fully — truly — comprehend. Why? Because from what I've seen, on earth and in "heaven", the universe contains no omniscient elements.

So, what are "we" humans? Who are we (I still, in a flowing sense, consider myself one)? The answer is really rather simple: Everything we do reveals what we are and who we are. We are creatures that believe in gods and origins and heavens and hells. We are creatures who build huts and houses and skyscrapers. We live and die like everything else. We have alphabets and languages and we use these to communicate with each other. We usually live in groups and we create states and nations that sometimes war with each other. We agree and disagree. When we disagree, we sometimes fight and even kill each other. We can be very cruel and we can be very loving. We have interesting astute minds that can build pyramids and travel to various places all over the earth in cars and airplanes now. (We will surely create new modes of transportation in the future.) We have even built rockets that can go to a distant moon that orbits our homeland, the place we call "the planet earth". Some of us exercise our bodies regularly and some of us don't. Some of us think a lot and others don't. We read and write and fall in love. We often seek wealth and live in ridiculously big houses. Others are content to live in tents or sleep in caves. We tend to eat animals (roughly 150,000,000 per day at this moment), but we are beginning to eat fewer and fewer as some of us have begun to value animals almost as much as ourselves. We like to play games and watch other people play games like football, tennis, and basketball. We sometimes conquer and kill. Sometimes we are sensitive and helpful. We have armies and hospitals, policemen, garbage collectors, and doctors. Now we have iPhones and computers and artificial "intelligence". We try to teach and learn things. For a couple millennia we have believed in concepts like justice, liberty, equality, and truth, yet we still have "national" boundaries and draw lines and sometimes won't let people pass. One of us once wrote, *There are churches, whorehouses, and McDonald's restaurants all over the planet. Need we know anything more to understand so-called 'human nature'?* ... Haha! Yes, I wrote that a long time ago! But what is time but a puff of smoke in our imaginations?

And so what is life? Life is all that is. Simple as that. And what is? I believe no one knows.

13

Earthly Creatures and the Struggle for Power

On that little earth, that I had the good fortune of being a part of, creatures (beings inside of Being) come and go. It seems (according to scientists) that at least 95% of all species that have been on the earth have disappeared long before humans started digging oil out of the ground, building big factories, and "polluting the planet". What people traditionally call "life" (breathing creatures like themselves) is the exception. Zillions of creatures have lived and died and returned to what my friend Tobey Hornato Beaman calls the "heart of Being" ("Grandma didn't die, she just returned to where she came from — the heart of infinite Being.").

Yes, earthly creatures are a fleeting part of Being. Nature changes. And one curious indelible aspect of nature is that some parts will always have more power than others. Some creatures will always rule. Some part of nature will always be eaten. The world will always be a jungle. And today, in that jungle, we humans have a certain degree of power. But having power is not "knowing what life is". The lion that munches on the leg of the dead antelope does not understand Being. Neither do the humans who control parts of our earth. Obviously, there is power that is kinder and gentler than other power. Will there ever be a consensus about how the world should operate? Will power ever bring lasting peace? No one knows. But one thing is certain. In nature there are nefarious parts and glorious parts. And all parts do what they do. And those parts that "think", will always do what they think they should do or not do. Every creature on Earth does what it thinks is "right" at every moment in time. And every other creature will judge what is right and wrong, or good or bad, based on his or her perspective and mind.

If I am right about the "fact" that nothing in the whole of Being can be other than what it is, then I herewith ask the same pertinent question Alfred E. Newman used to ask in *Mad Magazine* back in the days of my youth, i.e. "Why worry?" And the answer is obvious… Because the worriers can do nothing other. At least for now.

So let us resume. I believe existence is an unfathomable mystery. The fact that anything exists at all is mind-blowing. Consciousness is also mind-blowing. Consciousness allows existence to be perceived. Does human consciousness (or any consciousness) — and the so-called "mind" with which it is somehow connected — perceive existence ("reality") correctly? That too is a mystery. Of course, in almost all cases it thinks it does. Very few people question their own perceptions, thoughts, beliefs, and "truths". For me, no one knows what Being is. I tend to think it is infinite both temporally and spatially. That too is a mind-blowing thought. But we are alive. Yes! You and I and billions and billions of other creatures are alive. We all have our worlds and our cares. We all have our "truths". Most people's truths are the truths and "realities" of the day… of their time. Before we had the Greeks and their way of breaking the world into "mind and body", gods, morality, society, creation, free will, etc. Christianity stole much from the Greeks, but drew a picture of the universe with only one God on top of it all. The Hindus did otherwise with their bundle of gods. Islam kept the lone God but changed some of the rules of the game. Buddhists threw out the gods and tried to limit the suffering on Earth. Thanks to thinkers like Copernicus and Galileo, the earth was no longer the centre of the universe. But the God and the idea of creation perdured. Electricity was invented. Scientists of all kinds began creating wonderful machines that made everyday living easier. Agricultural practices and medical advances kept humans alive much longer than before. Nation states were everywhere. Borders changed many times. Warring was rather constant.

Nietzsche came along and said philosophy was mostly bullshit. God was no more real than Santa Claus and good and evil were not written into the fabric of existence. He called into question essentially all the truths and values of Western civilization. Two ugly world wars left a bloody stain on the 20th century. But technological progress was still incredible. And we got the computer and the smartphone. And so-called "Climate Change". But the world was surely a far more wonderful place for living than it had ever been before. Longevity went up everywhere. Fewer and fewer people were starving to death. Most people had water and a roof over their heads. Yes, the Covid crisis was a pain in the butt, but not all that many people died. Then the damn wars started in Ukraine and Israel (which ironically seemed to make people forget the wars in Korea, Vietnam, Iraq, Afghanistan, etc.), and many people couldn't agree on who was right and who was wrong… Well, I've been able to watch it all. You have too. And do you know what? I honestly believe none of it could have happened any other way. Yes! It's tragic. But there's also a hell of a lot of beauty in the mix…

Before I close this chapter, I'd like to chastise many people in Western civilization for bitching about everything all the time. You're like spoiled brats on Christmas morning who don't appreciate what they have and only complain about what they didn't get. But I won't really chastise you because I know you can be nothing other than who and what you are. You have the 24-hour news channels bashing all the horrors of the world in your face. And they can't be other than what they are. They're just "doing their job". And on and on the world goes round…

Let us feel the incredible mystery of all Being. And in so doing, let us have a deep respect for the existence of all things inside of Being. On Earth and in Heaven I have never known anyone who was in awe and wonder with regard to existence and who was not gentle at heart.

14

Once Upon Another Time

Once upon another time there was a man who turned to the world he wanted to change and declared, "Let us try to imagine a world wherein no one claims to know the truth about what life is all about, a world wherein no one claims to know what reality is, a world wherein no one is in a position to judge guilt and innocence, and a world wherein there is no hate and revenge because everyone realizes nothing can be other than what it is at every given moment in time!"

Now, the man knew myriads of others before him who had wanted to make the world a kinder gentler place, and probably most couldn't even make their own families a better place. Maybe he was such a person as well. Though he had tried to give love and goodness to his family, perhaps he too had failed. But on the other hand, maybe such judgements about success and failure were bogus. And it might be the case that a family is not a "thing" but is composed of many infinitely complex movable parts over which no one has ultimate control. Hence, wanting to help a family, friend, or a world might — in the end — boil down to the same thing and there is no reason not to try to bring about a little "goodness" and peace. The man's guiding principle had always been not to make things more difficult than they already were for every living creature that he came in contact with, human or otherwise, and, if possible, to bring joy to as many as possible. This applied for all situations. He couldn't kill a fly; he would always catch the spider in a jar and put it outside (always hoping it wasn't poisonous and would survive); he didn't ever remember being angry with his parents or friends; he could eat the chicken, but he could never kill it; if a woman he loved was unfaithful or left him, it hurt, but he never felt hate or anger towards her; he always tried to see the world from the point of view of the other person or creature; and he tried to befriend everyone and make peace whenever conflict arose…

… And until death, he continued to observe the world and all the beliefs that people had about truth and how the world worked. He noticed that organized religions were losing much of their clout, and that fewer people believed that there was a God or some such Jolly Green Giant "behind" the universe. Science was leaning toward a "Big Bang" or some similar "beginning", but for him the whole idea of a genesis made no sense whatsoever because in order to have a big bang, something had to exist to get "banged". In his mind, the only thing that made any sense was the idea that existence had always existed, but was constantly changing. He tended to doubt all people who thought there was a logic or intrinsic meaning behind Being. He believed everything was what it was and couldn't be anything other than what it was, a belief he still maintained and was convinced that its promulgation was the key to a better world.

And he thought that if he ever found God here, there, or everywhere, he would immediately ask two questions: "Dear God, was anything in the universe created in your image?" and "So, dear God, can anything in the universe be other than what it is, including You?" But he also had thought enough about things to know that if he ever found God, it would be very possible that God didn't speak English, or, for that matter, any language at all. He knew that maybe God and language had absolutely nothing to do with each other, and that if anything, He or She or It would be the first to know that language was simply a hammer and chisel that humans used to break the world into pieces so that they could play their little games of "Chutes and Ladders", "Monopoly", "King of the Mountain", "One Flew Over the Coo-coo's Nest", "Love Story", "The Ten Commandments", "Prison Break", "Gone with the Wind", etc., but that in the end language had nothing to do with what humans so presumptuously and naively called "reality" or "truth".

Yes, once upon a time, there was a man who thought that all that truth, reality, and the free will stuff had to go.

53

15

Am I Making My Point?
... Father Forgive Them

I want this story to be as limpid as possible. I want people to once and for all vanquish the idea that humans are "free" and act "freely", whereas the rest of the world is not "free" and acts "instinctively". I want people to understand that free will is a consummate error and that believers in free will (almost everybody in Western civilization) have created much of the pain and suffering in the world in the past and continue to do so today. By eliminating, now and forever, the idea that man is "free" (and the notion that man can know "truth" and "reality"), humanity will take a giant step towards a more peaceful planet.

Why? Because people like Epictetus (and me) never feel hate and a desire for vengeance when they see tragedy and ignorant deleterious actions by animals or humans. They are saddened by violence and suffering of all kinds. They try not to be a part of it, and they try to help others avoid it — just like we do with bad weather or venomous snakes or spiders. If possible, they always try to stop it when they see it. But, at the same time, they understand that not one single solitary creature in existence… in the whole damned or divine cosmos… "asked" to be what it is. Hence, they never get angry at their children because they know they are innocent. They help them, discipline them, and transmit values and an openness towards existence, but they never get mad at them or "punish" them. The same is true for everyone with whom they come in contact. They will try to correct harmful behavior, but they'll never seek vengeance upon its perpetrators. In understanding that all parts of being are what they are and can be nothing other at every given moment, their goal is always to help everyone move forwards in life, if possible, and they never want to hurt anyone or make life more difficult than it already is.

Am I making my point? When Jesus said, as he was dying on the cross, "Father, forgive them for they know not what they do," this was the greatest statement in the whole Christian Gospel. And yet few, if any, listened. Those who did, and took it to heart, have all been good people. Those who didn't listen and didn't adopt the idea to their way of life, have been part of what keeps the world from being a kinder gentler place. People who see human beings as being outside of nature, and hence potentially "evil", "punishable", etc. have never grasped Jesus's message.

Revenge and punishment have nothing to do with the Evangel of Christ. Concepts like good and evil, heaven and hell, and man and nature are dichotomies that have wreaked havoc on the mystery and beauty of the world.

16

The Heart of Lucidity

After watching human beings for a lifetime, I came to the conclusion that most people really do think existence exists for a "purpose" or a "reason".

At first glance this looks like a rather harmless thought. However, with a bit of reflection, it can reveal a huge problem. In fact, this propensity tends to turn "reality" — truth if you will — inside out.

Look more closely. When a human being thinks there is a reason "behind" existence, she or he sees everything through the lens (telescope, microscope, regular glasses, or eyes) of that purpose. A good Christian believes that God created the universe and he put us on Earth in order to test us such that after death we will be set somewhere for eternity. This amazing idea will influence everything about how a good Christian sees the world. Islam picked up on this idea and has a similar view of why existence exists. But what is important here is the idea that everything — absolutely everything — that these people see has a "logic" to it. Everything is interpreted to fit into a plan and has a meaning within that plan. Nothing exists outside that plan. When existence is reduced to a plan, it loses its lustre and wonder. When such a "mind" sees anything and everything, it always fits it into a place in a scheme of what existence (the world) is all about… and "should be". Even a scientist might do such a thing, i.e. see all being as something to be "understood" and will want theories to eventually "explain" everything on Earth and in the cosmos. A theist, on the other hand, will interpret everything that happens in the context of what divinity wants and expects. People with specific political persuasions naturally do the same kind of thing constantly. Psychologists and philosophers will fit everything that happens into their scheme. It seems that the human mind cannot help itself: it stamps a "logic" — a reason — on everything it encounters. Everything fits inside its weltanschauung. Even what the mind itself is will fit inside the mind.

So, I used to ask myself, "Whose way of seeing the world is right? Who has the correct way of interpreting and understanding what 'existence' is? Whose interpretation of Being is 'correct'?" In the West, Christianity and science have had the upper hand for millennia. In the East, Buddhism, Hinduism, Taoism, and science have reigned. In between the East and West, Islam and science have held the keys to what life is. Humanity everywhere has its way of giving a logic and interpretation to existence.

So, now where are we going... here... with this little book, written by a dead man in Never Everland? Perhaps to a place where very few people have ever gone. We are going to turn things inside out and imagine that everything in existence simply "exists" — is — and that nothing, absolutely nothing, exists for a reason or has a "logic" to it. Then we are going to grant the very real possibility that all human thinking (reason and logic) has nothing to do with "reality", but is simply the human way of making sense out of the great swirl of Being, but in so doing, often robs existence of its ineffable and unfathomable mystery and gleam.

Let us now for a moment imagine that every human idea about the existence of existence has been false, empty, and meaningless, that every galaxy, star, planet, moon, person, animal, insect, plant, molecule, atom, electron, quark, thought, mind, and brain simply are what they are and can be nothing other than what they are, and that there is no intelligent force "behind" anything, no reason, no logic, no purpose, and no "free will" anywhere in the cosmos! What then? Would this be a horrible thought or a wonderful thought? Would it be liberating or debilitating? Would it make the world better or worse? Ah! These are the questions we want to answer!

If (given no logic, purpose, or creator or free will)

human minds perceived everything in the universe to be as innocent as a newborn baby, kitten, planet, or flower, if all existence was blameless, guiltless, sinless, and pure (purely what it was and impossibly something other), if everything was "Mother Nature", wouldn't all hate and revenge disappear from the human comedy? Wouldn't an earth full of such lucid souls (like Epictetus and Jesus) simply want to make the world as happy and livable a place as possible? Wouldn't they look at the odious part of existence with minds devoid of any and all desire to hurt or punish, but simply with the desire to either change or eliminate them? They would surely never want to throw lightning bolts or condemn evil-doers to hell. They would surely not want to "punish" them and make them "suffer". They would constantly seek a world with as much joy as possible. Why would they want to do anything else?

And wouldn't this be the heart of lucidity?

17

What About the Other Characters in the Book?

Ah! What a wonderful question! Is this just my — William Winger's — one-man show with a mention here and there of Jesus and Epictetus? Where are the other characters in the story? Well, fellow cosmic dogpaddlers and lifeguards, the answer is simple: They are everywhere! Every human being you meet… every creature you see… every "thing" you see… All are part of this book! This book is about all existence!. The star of this book is all Being! The main characters are at every turn! Everywhere you look are the stars of the show!

I remember towards the end of my life on Earth, every person or creature I saw used to touch me to the bone. I always put myself in the other's shoes and realized that if I were them, I would be just like them. I thought of how every creature, human or otherwise, had to find a way to get through the day… to survive… to be "something" or "somebody". Every creature was important to itself. Every creature certainly wanted to be respected, or, dare I say, "loved". Or at least to have some grain of importance! I began to see every thread of existence as being sacred. And when the loving man on the cross whispered into the ear of humanity and said, "Father, forgive them for they know not what they do," I liked to think that I listened. At least I began to see every man, woman, child, animal, plant, star and moon as the most important character in the story.

18

A Brief Travel Guide to Nowhere and Everywhere

I have decided to write a travel guide about how to love the world. I woke up feeling fresh and well. (Yes, we still sleep in Never Everland.). It was a lovely day. It reminded me of spring on Earth when the sun would feel like a mother's warm hand on a cheek, arm, or belly.

I remembered an earthly friend, a woman named Judie Fein who loved the world, visited much of it, and wrote many books about her voyages and the myriads of wonderful human beings with whom she crossed paths. I thought it was my turn to tell a few tales about travel.

Point Number One. It doesn't matter where you go, there will always be something fascinating to see. Every trip I have ever taken has been an eye-opener. I was always seeing what we like to call "reality". How could reality not be fascinating? The traveller is reality and is confronting another reality. When realities mix there is always new reality. Every moment of every day — big travel or microscopic travel — is creating new reality.

Now, of course, the problem is that our brains might not be capable of ingesting, digesting, tasting, savouring, and appreciating what we are seeing. Some of us travellers will be judgemental and want to compare everything to what we are used to. If we do so, we will make immediate and biased decisions about what is "good" and "bad" based on what we have lived in our lives. We will be incapable of appreciating people and things that do not correspond to what we ourselves consider to be the way the cosmos should be. What we must realize, if we want to be real "travellers", is that there is no such thing as "how the cosmos should be"! Being is what it is everywhere. It is what it is for a million reasons that none of us can understand. A real traveller will always look at what she or he sees with awe and wonder.

So what is the opposite of a real traveller? A bogus traveller? A limited traveller? A close-minded traveller? An Ugly American, or Ugly European, or Ugly Asian, or Ugly African? (Certainly, small-mindedness can come from any part of the world.) And should such travellers be "blamed" for being who they are? Of course not. None asked to have the brains, bodies, or experiences they have had. We are not here to rant against such people. All we want to do is to get people to open to the newness that travel can bring. And newness can bring freshness. Freshness can bring joy. Joy can bring new reasons to live. And one new reason to live can be to feel the complexity of existence and look at it with awe and wonder instead of "good" and "bad".

In our case, everywhere we have travelled in the cosmos has helped open our minds to the complexity of reality. We have become so open that we have stopped judging even the most primitive peoples or the most blockheaded chauvinistic creatures that inhabit the earth.

We have travelled space enough to know life's greatest secret: Nothing can be other than what it is at any moment in time. And in reality, there is no time; there is only the stuff of being that is constantly changing.

Amen.

There is no Point Number Two, or Three, or Twenty-Seven.

19

A Letter of Apology
to Gustav and Egon

Speaking of travel, one day way back when, I took a little trip to Vienna. When I got home, I wrote this letter to two men who were long dead. Actually, I bumped into both Gustav and Egon not long ago. We had a good laugh. They were not quite sure how they got my letter, but they did. When we were talking, the subject of art as a form of necessary masturbation came up, and the possibility that everything in the cosmos was "instinctive". They both said they couldn't disagree. Anyway, here's the letter I penned shortly after the trip. Amazingly, Gustav had it in the front left pocket of his tattered jeans…

Dear Gustav and Egon,

You have both been dead now for a hundred and one years. I have lived during the last sixty of those years. It is high time I apologize to both of you.

Until a week ago, I never appreciated you. I was an unseeing unthinking idiot. My opinion about you was totally false. I was unappreciative of your genius. I had a stupid prejudice against you for three reasons. First, I tended to dislike paintings with people in them. I saw enough people every day. I liked abstraction and colour in painting. I liked painting that was different from what I saw in the world. The second reason is that almost every time I saw a reproduction of one of your paintings in a magazine, book, or newspaper, it was the famous "Kiss" painting, the one with the gold leafing and the couple embracing. I saw it a thousand times. I thought you, Gustav, were "commercial". I thought you were shallow, sloppy, romantic, and somehow just out to sell your stuff. And dumbly I put you Egon in the same basket. Thirdly, I have lived in Switzerland for many years and always seen Paris as "the place to be". I had never been to Vienna and in my university years French culture had been number one on the intellectual hit parade, i.e. Sartre's "No Exit", Camus' "The Stranger" and "The Plague", Flaubert's "Madame Bovary and "The Sentimental Education", Levi-Strauss's anthropology, Stendhal's "The Red and the Black", Van Gogh's death in southern France was somehow cool, Delacroix was French, André Gide and Cocteau were French, Picasso had spent most of his life in France, the Boulevards St. Michel and St. Germaine were cool, Notre Dame was the church of churches, the Louvre had the Mona Lisa, and of course Montmartre, that little hill next to the Sacré

Coeur, was home to so many "must-see" painters, i.e. people with names that sounded like prophets — Degas, Matisse, Renoir, Toulouse-Lautrec, Utrillo, Modigliani, Monet, Mondrian, and Steinlen. That was where I wanted to be. That was where the action was.

So, for years and years I went to France whenever I could. I ate French food and drank French wine; I watched films by Godard, Truffaut, Renoir, and Resnais; I wandered the Bourgogne countryside, and drove down to the Riviera. I had been sucked into thinking that France was the cultural and intellectual capital of the world. Of course New York was cool, but for me, an American, it was never as cool as Paris.

I rarely went to Germany and I never went to Austria. The Germanic world was somehow second-rate. Klimt and Schiele couldn't box in the same ring with Cézanne and Gauguin. Only Nietzsche was the exception. But hadn't he tossed German culture in the garbage bin? Of course I knew Freud was from Vienna. But at a rather early age I thought Freud was full of baloney (actually I still pretty much do). I never wanted to make love to my mother or kill my father. I had no idea what an "ego" was, much less a "subconscious". For me "consciousness" has always been one of the greatest mysteries of all and I always thought the "subconscious" was so deep and went back so far, that it was ridiculous to even think we could begin to understand it. And yes, I had read Kafka. I never forgot the man who became a bug or the man never knowing why he was on trial, but it just wasn't enough to get me to Vienna. As for Mozart, somehow I associated him more with Salzburg than Vienna and getting to Salzburg always seemed like a complicated affair.

Other than my many trips to Paris, I did find time to go to London, Bath, Edinburgh, Rome, Venice (five times at least), Sorrento, Milan, Budapest, Brussels, Oostende, Amsterdam, Barcelona, Seville, Madrid, Palma, Antalya, Marrakesh, Hammamet, Bangkok, Phuket, Hong Kong, Copenhagen, Malmö, and Heidelberg.

But life seemed too short to go to Austria…

O what a fool I was! Last week I finally went to Vienna. I have my family to thank. A three-day trip was my birthday present. Probably the best present I've ever got in my life. I want you to know that today it might be my favorite city in the world for a hundred reasons. But two of those reasons are you, you Gustav Klimt and you Egon Schiele. Your paintings pierced my skin, set fire to my frazzled soul, played hopscotch with my battered brain, and brought tears to my weary eyes. I saw your works at the Belvedere, Leopold, and Albertina museums. Everything was beautifully presented. Beauty, life, guts, joy, mystery, suffering, infinity. It's all there. I now consider you two of the greatest painters ever to have lived.

This is not the time or the place to analyze your work and your genius. What I want to say here is that I am sorry for being so small-minded for so many years with regard to who you were, what you lived, and how you

*painted. My stupid uninformed prejudices had kept me
away from your glorious work and your beautiful city.
It is that way for so many things in life.
Sincerely and humbly,*

William Winger   December 13, 20——

When Gustav folded the letter up and stuck it back in
his pocket, I saw Egon had a tear in the corner of an
eye. Nothing could have made me happier.

20

Ants

I love ants almost as much as I love all other legged creatures except dogs, cats, and people. I have loved them halfway to eternity. Here too they are everywhere.

I respect ants as much as I respect all other creatures.

I care about the life and death of each ant even though there are about 10,000,000,000,000,000 of them on the earth alone, not to speak of the rest of the cosmos. I do not believe that when a species is numerous it diminishes the value and importance of the individual. The facts that there are one million humans or eight billion humans changes nothing about the value of each life. Each is the most important life to itself and should be appreciated as such by other lucid creatures. Also, the size of a creature does not influence my feeling about its importance. I can see no logical justification for valuing large creatures over small creatures. Ants and elephants are both marvellous and magnificent. What does size mean when space is infinite?

I still cannot put myself in the mind of an ant and I doubt an ant could put itself in my mind. I have no idea if ants respected me when I was alive, even while I was showing Laura how to step carefully over them. In any case, ants and I will never have a perfect knowledge of each other. For that matter, it is very unlikely that any two creatures ever have a perfect knowledge of each other.

Once, a very long time ago, I had a run-in with a community of ants. I have no idea how many I maimed or killed. Here is what happened:

I had to clean an outside drain. To get to the drain, it was necessary to open a double window in a little-used room in our basement. The room was full of cobwebs. I vacuumed the cobwebs and dust and then pried open the window. There were hundreds of ants running back and forth along the windowsill, which was covered with silt and grime. The ants began running frenetically as I cleared away the dirt and cleaned the debris around the drain. I had obviously interrupted the routine of whatever they had been doing. They came out of the aging woodwork like an unending troop of wild soldiers and started storming into the room where I was standing. I quickly closed the window, but they kept coming. I felt I had no choice. I started vacuuming them.

I was using an old machine that we keep in the

basement. It still had the power to suck in most of what vacuums are supposed to guzzle. The ants didn't stand a chance…but they kept coming. Hundreds of them. I kept vacuuming, all the while asking their forgiveness and feeling like a filthy assassin. No, they had done nothing to deserve such a fate. Yes, sometimes one is forced to make horrible choices. Should I let the ants parade into the basement or should I eliminate them? I had to make a quick decision. I didn't really want a slew of ants in the house and I don't think Laura or her mom did either.

I got almost all that had come into the room. I sensed that the vacuum sack was full. Could the ants live for a while in the bag or would they all have perished as they flew up the vacuum tube? I decided to empty the bloated sack outside into the large green bin for "natural" garbage…

I began pulling the debris out with my fingers. To the delight of my moral conscience, ants began scurrying everywhere in the mess below my eyes. Had they all survived? I emptied the bag and left the lid of the garbage bin open in case the ants wanted to leave. I was deeply relieved, but many questions remained unanswered… Would the ants feel uprooted from their "home" inside the windowsill in the mulch and rotting wood? Would they miss the others? Would the others miss them? Were homesickness and loneliness emotions ants had to deal with? Could ants feel disoriented? To what extent do ants "feel" anything?

Could they somehow find their way back to the others (the bin was about fifteen metres from the window)? Would they find a new life in the garbage? What would happen on Tuesday when the big city trucks came by and emptied my three green bins? Could the ants survive in that jungle of junk? In any case, I remembered reading that the life span of worker ants was a few weeks at most, though queen ants could live up to fifteen years. What if I had killed a queen...?

On and on my mind wandered thinking about the fate of these ants, then all ants, and, eventually, all living beings.

Yes, it is impossible to live a moral life.

21

A Sudden Calm

And me? Am I still a living being, strutting about on the stage of life? When I lived and loved with Laura's mother, I was the king of the cosmos. It was the greatest love, the kind that completely fills your being, when you "can't live" without the other and you go crazy when you are separated, when you crave for the next moment you are together and you constantly want to "make love", and when you do make love you don't want to stop, etc... It was the kind of love that incessantly wants more! When it ended with her death, I was foolish enough to want it back, to think I could find it again, if not on Earth, then in Heaven. Yes. there was a part of me that always thought the hole in the heart would be filled again. I never told anybody, but that was part of the reason I put a hole in my brain. The pancreatic cancer was causing great pain, but there was also the aching in the heart...

And even here, I kept looking, wandering, wondering if I would find it again. Suddenly, yesteryear, I didn't seek it anymore. I stopped missing the feeling, the adrenaline, the company, the craving, and the mad lovemaking. Existence became a movie I was watching and was amused by. But I was no longer an actor, no longer the star of the show, no longer the hero who would hold the woman of his dreams in his arms and passionately kiss her as the words "The End" flash on the screen. I suddenly realized that perhaps it really was the end — the real end of ends. There was a wave of calm on the cosmic shore. I accepted the idea that great love would never come my way again, and that I might as well accept my fate, like my friend Manuel accepted the fact that he was going blind and there was nothing the doctors of the world could do about it. In my case, I was accepting an eternal emptiness wherein the bonfire of mad love would never burn again as there was nothing left to incinerate and no one to strike the match.

22

Saving Grace

I have said it a thousand times, but since nobody listens, I'll say it again: The most fascinating flagrant telling "fact" (I use the word lightly of course) about human beings is that they cannot step back and feel the unfathomable mystery of existence, i.e. that existence exists... that something... anything... exists at all. It is all mind-blowing. But human minds don't get blown because people all grow up in a culture (society, civilization) that has some kind of explanation for where everything came from, what everything "is", what is important, and what is good and what is not. Every society does this. Any social scientist or philosopher can tell you this. But do they ever get their minds blown by existence? Or are they too not trapped in a civilization and too busy being "thinkers" (or fathers, mothers, lovers, breadwinners, etc.) to step back and grasp the inscrutable mystery of Being?

Language doesn't help either. It too helps conceal

the mystery. As soon as we are old enough to crawl and babble, the people around us are teaching us words for the things we see and touch and for what is going on around us. And on it goes... We naturally think these words are describing the world and "reality". Of course they aren't, but we are too dumb to know it, and the sad truth is that most of us spend our whole earthly lives being too dumb to know that language does not describe reality...

But wait! Perhaps this is not a "sad" truth, but rather a "saving truth". Yes! That is what I really believe. The fact that 99.99% of humanity cannot grasp the unfathomable mystery of existence is what keeps civilization going. If ants were thinking about the unfathomable mystery of being, do you think they could create all the wonderful anthills they make? The same is true for humans... We could not make all the wonderful things we make if we were obsessed with the mystery of Being.

And if our bluntness was our saving grace?

23

Art and Artists

love going through my attic of memories — things I've written, letters received, articles collected — and finding tidbits like this. What is eternal death if not a pile of remembrances and a few hopes and expectations? …

Though I have painted for thirty years and written many novels since 19——, I have never referred to myself as "an artist". When I hear the word "art" I have always tended to think the speaker to be either pretentious or a shallow thinker or both. Questions like "What is art?", "What is the purpose of art?", and "What is the role of art in the world?" have always left me cold primarily because art itself has never been properly defined.

Art is often associated with creation and expression. It also seemingly implies a notion of "free will". A snail that creates a silver trail on a sidewalk is not normally referred to as an artist. Birds singing in trees don't get the adoration of a Renata Tibaldi or a Joan Sutherland.

Animals are not granted the status that humans are, to wit "free". Animals are said to act instinctually whereas humans are supposed to have the capacity to "think" and "choose" and such. When a bird builds a nest, nobody talks about "architecture". A monkey swinging from branch to branch isn't doing "ballet".

So, my guess is that humans use the term "art" to feel good about themselves. They get to rise out of the jungle. Like with most religions, they get to feel that on the totem pole of existence they sit "just a notch below God".

This is all baloney. I don't think we're free. I don't think human behaviour is any less instinctual than animal behavior. I think to separate man from the animal world is ridiculous.

In my own case I have noticed that when I write novels and paint pictures I do so not because I "want to", but because I "have to". If I'm not writing a novel or preparing a paint show I go crazy. My acts of creation are no more acts of free will than a dolphin's leaps in the ocean or a snail's silver trail on a sidewalk. I never consider myself to be doing "art"; I consider myself to be being what I am and doing what I have to do.

As a result, I have tended to throw terms like art and creation into the garbage can... Until, that is, the eighth of August, 20———. On this day at about five o'clock in the afternoon, I used the word "art" and gave "art" a reason to exist.

It was the last day of the family vacation. We had spent a week in Corsica — four days in and around

Bonifacio and three days in Ajaccio. We were flying out the next morning.

Though I've lived in Switzerland for decades and decades, I had never been to Corsica before. I had heard the people were not particularly friendly, that there was too much traffic, and had thought, "why go to Corsica when you can go to….?" Well, you finish the sentence. I had been dumbed with my dumb prejudices. Actually, we had wanted to go to Mallorca (where we'd already been three times), but the easyJet ticket prices to Palma were three times more expensive when I started looking for a warm summer destination. Ajaccio was sixty francs each way, cheaper than taking the train from Lausanne to Zurich.

Corsica was the opposite of everything I had expected. It was not crowded, the people were wonderful, and the island is as beautiful as the world gets. The only problem for me was that there is only one golf course, Sperone. But it is such a great course — the Pebble Beach of Europe — that I will forgive the Corsicans their lack of interest in my favourite pastime at age sixty-one.

By the last day I was "beached-out" and my skin told me "no more sun, please, kind sir." It was four o'clock. I had just taken a nap. The "family" wanted to go to the pool in our Best Western hotel. I picked up the tourist map of the Ajaccio area and saw there was a museum just a couple of blocks away called "Le Musée Marc Pétit". I knew the area because I had gone alone to the beach there the first morning for a swim at sunrise. (The *family always gets up much later than I do on vacation. I drink wine at night and go to bed early. They drink Coke and ice tea and watch TV until around midnight.) There was a big ugly apartment "résidence" next to the beach of Aspretto and the water was not the turquoise Tahiti blue we had seen in Bonifacio. But I had enjoyed the swim.*

Anyway, looking at the map I knew more or less where the museum was and it was only a five-minute walk from the hotel…

I crossed the busy four-lane road that runs along the bay, walked past the ugly building, looked down at the beach — it was crowded in the afternoon — and kept plodding along the rather trashy cracked sidewalk. Suddenly there was a nice yellow house on the left side of the road. It had an open driveway. Part of it said "residence privé" and part said "Musée Marc Pétit". I read the small print on the sign out front and learned that the house had been used to quarantine cholera victims in the eighteenth and nineteenth centuries. When the cholera epidemic was pretty much over, a rich family bought the building and certain surviving members still lived there. They loved the French sculpture named Marc Pétit and had bought a slew of his works.…

I took five steps up the driveway. The grass in front of the private residence was the green of cooked broccoli. Gleaming green, canary yellow, cobalt sky: art anybody?… Straight ahead of me was a gravel path with a line of sculptures. Marc Pétit had definitely seen

Giacometti. The first had a skinny man with tree branches coming out of his upper body. Great stuff. The next was what looked like a child's playpen full of emaciated standing humans with skulls with no eyes or mouths or noses. Ten metres further there was a living young woman sitting in the shade of the building in a fold-out chair. She stood up. 28 maybe. Nice wavy brown hair. Light brown eyes. Asked me if I wanted to see the exhibition. What exhibition? The one inside the building... It's a twentieth century Expressionist exhibition chosen by Marc Pétit. Is he still alive? Yes... and if you want to look at the sculptures first, they go around the building. Thanks, I said.

The sculptures and the garden were perfect for each other. There were orange, red, and yellow flowers everywhere. All the sculptures were of skinny people who looked lonely or suffering or both.

The young woman took me inside the part of the building where the paintings were. I only had nine euros in my pocket and a ticket was ten. She let me slide. I asked her if I had been her only customer that day. The answer was yes.

I knew Zoran Music's work. I had seen pieces in Paris and Lausanne. I didn't know the other three painters. One painted what appeared to be mentally struggling men hunched over holding their penises. I told the woman I preferred paintings without people in them. She talked about human solitude and what Marc Pétit had in common with the men who had painted all the pictures I was looking at.

When we got back outside for some reason I said, "The only reason for art is to take people out of the humdrum of their everyday lives and to get them to feel the incredible mystery of existence." I surprised myself because I had used the words "art" and "reason for".

The young woman didn't say anything to my remark. She did say she had studied art history at the university in Corti. We talked. She followed me down to the end of the garden.

I had been there an hour. I needed to get back to my wife and daughter.

We went to dinner that last night in the old town of Ajaccio.

Best pizza I ever had in my life.

24

Box of Surprises

I've been dead for what seems like half an eternity. In human time it probably hasn't even been a decade. I always look back on my terrestrial life with awe and wonder. What a world. What a circus. What a bizarre bazaar. The truth is that everything and nothing surprised me. Mass murders didn't surprise me; what surprised me was that there weren't more of them. Floods didn't surprise me; what surprised me was that with all the water out there that there weren't more of them. Wars didn't surprise me; what surprised me was that, in the West at least, they had been rather scarce towards the end of my time on Earth. No suicide ever surprised me, including my own; what surprised me was that with all the tragedy and suffering in the world, people didn't knock themselves off more often. Bad drivers didn't surprise me; what surprised me was that in spite of the fury of the modern world, most people were actually rather good, considerate drivers. If something went wrong in a human body, I was never shocked; I was shocked that human bodies — and animal and plant bodies — functioned so miraculously well most of the time. When somebody went off his or her rocker, or had a panic attack in an airplane, I was not at all astounded; I was astounded at how rarely someone acted like an idiot in an airplane (given the way we were sardine-packed in those flying machines) and how the majority of my fellow human beings were quite civil, polite, and even-keeled.

Of course, there were exceptions, but generally the world functioned astonishingly well, just like anthills and beehives did. Cities all over the world always amazed me. In places like Paris, Bangkok, Copenhagen and Vienna, people basically got along with each other. Things worked. Bodies and machines functioned. Buildings stayed up. In all my visits to these cities, I saw no dead people, no overt violence, no traffic accidents, no electricity breakdowns, and actually I never even saw anybody yelling at anybody else. The same was true for the time I spent in Munich, Brussels, London. Venice, Lisbon, San Francisco, Hong Kong, Lausanne, and Zurich.

But I also remember how hordes of people liked to bitch and complain about the world. They had no perspective on what life had been like in the past. Not me. I appreciated the world… even praised it… eventually to high heaven… literally. But, of course, I was fortunate to have lived in places that were never at war. In my sixty-plus years on Earth I never saw a human being kill another human being in real life. I knew it went on, but I never witnessed it. I saw millions of people in many different countries in many corners of the world, but I never actually saw a person get killed. Those bodies of ours functioned amazingly well. Apart from my beloved wife, I never witnessed anybody else actually passing from the state of being alive to the state of being dead. Though I was not a big fan of elevators, I was never in an elevator that got stuck. I rode in hundreds of airplanes, but never in one that crashed or had to make an emergency landing. I was never physically attacked (except by myself to end my life), though once at 5a.m. in New York City a guy tried to steal my bag, but I held on tightly and he got scared and ran away. And only twice in fifty years of driving cars did one break down on me and stop.

Yes, the world functioned amazingly well while I was riding on it. As I watch it now from afar, I still wish people would stop bitching about everything so much. That was why I hated 24-hour news channels. The majority of the time they talked about the horrors of the world. But I — like my gentle mother — used to say, "Count your blessings you ungrateful bastards." And count other people's blessings too. Of course, there are tragedies daily and some shitty places to live on Earth. But things are a whole lot better than they used to be. The planet Earth has never been a Garden of Eden, and never will be for that matter! It's been a place where things come to life and then die. The cosmos is still a total mystery, even from where I am now. I still think that it never came to be, but has always existed. As far as I'm concerned, that's the only thing that makes any sense. And, thanks to consciousness… that little mysterious light inside us all… we're aware that something is there and we are a part of it.

Okay, go ahead and complain and bitch if you want. If that's the way you are, then that's the way you are. But I'll stick to my amazement and awe about how incredible it all is. I'm sure Laura will too. And because I stopped believing in free will a half an eternity ago, I just see all you whiners and naysayers as natural parts of the big box of surprises.

25

So Where Do We Go from Here?

I am convinced that the more people come to see existence like I do, the greater the chances for peace on your wild wonderful Earth — and maybe even in eternity's ineffable infinite garden. When Jesus uttered that single sentence, "Father forgive them, for they know not what they do," as he was agonizing on the cross (assuming that's what really happened more than two thousand human years ago), there was a presumption that nothing in all of Being could be other than what it was at any given moment.

Yes, the world has been what it has been, is what it is, and will be what it will be. I know that I — the man called "William Winger" when he was part of the human herd — am but a tiny cog in the great wheel of Being. I am one of those odd rare pieces that does not believe in free will and who thinks, for all the reasons put forth in this little book, that slipping humankind back into the belly of mother nature will eventually be the key to a better world, to a more agreeable existence wherever existence and consciousness exist!

And another part of a better world would be for human beings to finally realize something that took death for me to understand: that we are all full of bullshit! Laura saw it before I did!

When I finally woke up from the dead and stepped back and looked at the world from afar, I realized that the human mind puts its stamp on everything. Without the human mind there would be no names for anything. No place on the earth would have a name. No part of existence would have a name or identity. Everything on the earth (and in the "known" cosmos for that matter) is what it is because the human mind says it is. Without the human mind, nothing in all of Being would have an identity. The human mind has put labels on everything, i.e. on everything it thinks needs a label. It breaks everything into pieces of a puzzle (existence!) and then puts it back together again and thinks it has made sense of… what is… so-called "Being". From here… from the point of view of a dead man… the whole thing is laughable. It is a gargantuan joke. Human beings stamp everything they can get their eyes, hands, and minds on with a label of "truth". If we could all step back and realize that this is what we have been doing for as long as we can remember, and that none of it is really true, life on Earth could become one great gratuitous party! We exist! Merci! Basta!

And as for the title of this book, *Don't Bullshit Me*

God, I love it as much as I love you readers for following me to the end. Of course, I stole it from Laura who wrote *Don't Bullshit Me Daddy* and *Don't Bullshit Me Johnny* some moons ago… moons I have no need to count now. But God hasn't bullshitted anybody. How could a being whose existence has never been defined or confirmed do such a thing? No, God has never been a bullshitter. He didn't need to be. His self-anointed children have done it all for Him.

26

The Telling Part of the Tale

And now, as we bring our story to a close, I want to touch on one last thing with regard to the earth and its passengers. One day, perhaps a quarter of an eternity ago, as I was reading the works of Nobel prize winner John Coetzee, I suddenly realized that after hundreds of pages I had hardly smiled or chuckled once. Then I thought, "The same has been true for other Nobel prizewinners I've read! Few laughs or smiles. What kind of a world is this? Where is the joy, the levity, the gaiety, and the pure appreciation that anything exists at all and that all of us are part of it!"

And now I have realized that I have been somewhat a part of that over-seriousness in the opus you are holding in your hands, my own *Don't Bullshit Me God*. More than anything, it is a homage to my dear daughter Laura who lost both her mother and father before she had lived eighteen years on the earth. And yet she was able to keep a smile on her face and write two books full of a certain joy, happiness, and appreciation for life! In my case, if I didn't leave the world on a happy note, at least I want to leave eternity on one.

Today, human scientists are saying that there are more galaxies in the universe than stars in our galaxy, and it is estimated that there are between 100 and 400 billion stars in our quaint little Milky Way. That means there are (perhaps, of course) more than 100,000,000,000 — or even 400,000,000,000 — GALAXIES! Each with some 250,000,000,000 (if we take the average) stars in them! Oh Lordy me! And to think people used to say the USA, China, Russia, and Brazil were "big places"!

What I'm trying to say is that with a little perspective we can laugh at just about everything. That is the telling part of the tale. We don't laugh enough. We don't smile enough. We take ourselves much too seriously. And that's what I love about Laura. Anybody who can write a book called *Don't Bullshit Me Daddy* has a sense of humour. So Laura, this book is dedicated to you, and every other part of the universe that can look around itself, into the depths of infinity, and say "Don't bullshit me God", and then grin.

Find out more about Jon Ferguson
and his works at his author website:
www.jonfergusonbooks.com,
where you can also sign up for updates.

Please contribute an honest online review;
it's the easiest and most supportive thing a reader can do
for an author and/or a small independent press.
editor@hugejam.com

www.ingramcontent.com/pod-product-compliance
Lightning Source LLC
Chambersburg PA
CBHW032020180726
48283CB00008B/2758